Christmas in Hartford

G.P. Jackson

Geletta Shavers

Copyright © 2025 by G.P. Jackson

All rights reserved.

No portion of this book may be reproduced in any form without written permission from the publisher or author, except as permitted by U.S. copyright law.

The names, characters, events, business, and incidents in this book are fictitious or inspired by the author's imagination. None of the characters in this book are based on an actual person. Any resemblance to persons living or dead is entirely coincidental and unintentional.

Contents

Dedication		VII
1.	The Night Everything Changed	1
2.	The Call	6
3.	The Hartford Inn	11
4.	The Coffee Shop	16
5.	The Christmas Market	20
6.	Christmas Pies	25
7.	The Date	32
8.	Art and Pastries	39
9.	The Christmas Mixer	46
10.	More Pies	51
11.	The Surprise	54
12.	The Gala	57

13. Falling Hard	62
14. Christmas Eve	66
15. New Year's Day	75
Epilogue- Coming Next Christmas in Hartford Wedding	83
About the author	90

Dedication

I dedicate this book to Anthony Hester, my youngest child's father. The man who reminded me that real love is gentle, patient, kind, and worth believing in.B efore Anthony, I had stopped trusting in relationships, stopped hoping for something lasting.Then, he walked into my life, loved my children like his own, and even opened his heart to my four-legged baby.

He showed me what it felt like to be cherished, to be chosen, and to know I was worthy of a love that didn't hurt. Though life took us down different roads after ten years of marriage, our friendship never wavered. Love transformed into something different, but it never disappeared.

The Night Everything Changed

I used to believe you got married and stayed married forever. That's what my parents did. They've been going strong for fifty-seven years. When I married Jeremy, I thought sharing my life and my law firm was what love and commitment looked like. I built Thompson Law Firm from scratch, long before I became Mrs. Jeremy Johnson. It was my dream, my legacy. But when we got married, I made him my partner and changed the firm's name to Thompson & Johnson.

He had only passed the bar two years before, but I told myself marriage meant fifty-fifty. What was mine was ours.

We were happy in love. I stopped my birth control because we were trying to start a family. He was my everything. That's what I believed until five years ago today.

I remember it as if it were yesterday. Since my business trip to New York was canceled at the last minute, I planned to surprise my husband, the love of my life. I drove out of my way to Big Daddy's Bar and Grill to pick up his favorite smash cheeseburger and onion rings and headed to the office. It was 9:30 p.m., but the lights were still on.

There were two cars in the parking lot; one was Jeremy's, and the other looked familiar. I brushed it off because he told me he would be working late tonight on the Alexander case. When I walked into the building, I heard heavy moaning. My heart sank into my stomach before my brain could process what I was hearing. My face twisted with confusion, anger, and disbelief. Following the moans straight to his office, I pushed open the door, and there he was.

"Jeremy!" I screamed with disgust and threw the food across the office.

He jumped up, scrambling to explain. I didn't need him to explain anything to me. I knew exactly what was happening.

"Jeremy, I can't believe what I'm seeing!" I screamed, and tears streaked down my face like a fast, angry river.

He stammered, trying to pick up his pants, almost tripping from the shock of me catching him in the act. "Honey, I'm sorry. I know I'm wrong for this. I don't know what I was thinking. You know this isn't me. I love you!"

He moved from the couch, and that's when I saw her face. "Carol? What the hell?" My administrative assistant.

Rage took over me. "Carol, pick up your underwear and get out of this building! You're fired, and I will have your things delivered to your apartment!"

"Listen, Jenny, this just happened. Please forgive me; you know I've been going through it since I had to place my mother in the nursing home." Her eyes darted to the floor, then the window as she shifted her weight from one foot to the other while putting on her underwear.

"You were more than my assistant; you were my friend. You've been with me since the beginning. I can't look at either of you. Get out now!"

Carol ran out with her shoes in hand, and I lost it. I tore through Jeremy's office, tossing files, papers, anything I could grab, while he babbled apologies. "It was a onetime thing," he said. "It just happened, Jenny. I'm so sorry."

"I don't care. We're done. I want a divorce," I screamed, my chest heaving as the words tore out of me.

He had raised his hands as if he were warding off gunfire, and I kept flinging everything within reach at him, my vision blurred with fury and tears. Then I stormed out, sat in my office, and called my best friend, Tanya. I could barely get the words out through the tears.

That was five years ago. Today, Carol and Jeremy are getting married. She's pregnant with triplets, no less.

So here I was. I took Tanya up on her invitation to visit her hometown in Hartford, Connecticut, for the holidays. The plan was to stay there for a month.

Jeremy refused to let me buy him out of the firm. Since the business and our reputations were intertwined, the judges in Chicago made it clear: we'd have to work it out ourselves. This meant I was forced to see him every single day.

He rehired her, and she's now one of our paralegals. Tanya gave me some kneepads for my birthday. I looked at her with a quizzical expression and asked what they were for, and she laughed, saying she knew I needed them because I stayed on my knees praying for the strength to deal with Jeremy and Carol. Once they got married, my former assistant, who helped ruin my life, would own half of what I built before I met Jeremy. They'd better be happy I was a Christian because anyone else would burn this building down with them in it for all they put me through.

My sense of powerlessness over the situation stung me to my core. But this holiday season, I was taking a break and practicing self-care for my peace of mind. My paralegals and associates could handle my caseload. This lawyer was officially off duty. I was packing up, heading to Hartford, and praying that peace or maybe something resembling peace was waiting for me there.

The Call

Two hours before Jeremy's wedding, my phone rang. *It's him. Why would he be calling me on his wedding day?* I almost didn't answer. He was the last person I expected to hear from. For all I knew, he was probably going to ask me to serve the food at their reception. It wouldn't be far-fetched with all the accommodating I'd been doing to keep a peaceful work environment.

My thumb hovered over the Answer button. *Don't answer it. It's probably some nonsense.* But the phone kept vibrating in my hand. What if it's important? What if something happened at the firm?

Against my better judgment, I swiped to answer, jabbing the screen harder than necessary.

"What is it?"

"Jenny," he said softly. His voice still held the calm, professional tone I once found sexy and comforting. The same one that now made my skin crawl. "I just wanted to say I'm sorry. For everything. For how things worked out between us and for hurting you."

I took a deep breath, fighting the anger in my body. "Jeremy, why do you think it's a good idea to call me today of all days?"

He fell silent.

"Do you even realize what today is?" I asked, my voice sharp. "It's five years to the damn day that I walked into your office and caught you and Carol..." I stopped myself before the memory could spill out completely, and I lost it on him again.

He sighed. "I didn't realize the date, Jenny. I swear I didn't."

I let out a big laugh; I couldn't help it. "Of course, you didn't. You never realize anything until it's too late."

He tried again, with that soft tone still in place. The one he used to manipulate me.

"I just wanted you to know that I never meant to hurt you. Things happened so fast. Carol's pregnant now with triplets, and, well, we can't stay in the townhouse anymore."

My jaw tightened. I didn't like where this conversation was going.

"So," he continued, "I was wondering if you'd consider selling me the house. The one we built together. It's got five bedrooms. It would be perfect for me, Carol, and the babies. It's just you, and you don't need all that space. I'll be doing you a favor."

When he stopped speaking, I went still, steadying myself before responding to that rancid, gutter-bred excuse for an offer. He had lost his mind!

"Excuse me?" My voice rose along with my eyebrows. "You want me to sell you the house we built together, the same house I designed and decorated so you and your mistress, turned wife, can raise your triplets there? Jeremy, you're awfully close to the edge and I'm willing to push you over, watch your body fall to the bottom, and not shed a tear. That's what I think about your offer. Hell no!"

"Jenny, it's just a house."

"No," I snapped. "It's not just a house. It's a reminder of everything I built, just like the law firm you're still working at. My law firm. The one I brought you into when you barely passed the bar exam. The firm I created from the ground up while you were still figuring out how to draft a motion."

"Come on, Jenny, be reasonable. You have no use for a house this big and...!"

"No!" I cut him off. "You won't let me buy you out of the business so I don't have to see you and her every day, but now you want to buy me out of my home? So, you and Carol can play house? Not happening, Jeremy! The gall of you!"

He didn't say a word. I could hear church music in the background. The wedding guests were arriving. All the laughter, chatter, and the sound of his new life beginning while mine was crumbling.

I took a deep breath and, with a genuine spirit and the Lord's help, said these words to the man who ruined my life. "I wish you well in your marriage. But I will not let you or Carol ruin another part of my life. I've spent five years picking up the pieces. I'm done letting your choices control me."

"But Jenny..."

"I'm through with this conversation," I said firmly. "The paralegals and associates can handle anything that comes up at the firm. I'm taking time off for myself and finding tranquility and peace in Hartford with Tanya. Don't call me again."

Before he could say another word, I pressed End on my phone, and it felt exhilarating. I didn't feel anger toward him. I felt relief. Maybe I'd forgiven them.

I looked out my window and saw the beautiful snowflakes falling, coating my lawn. It seemed like God had given me a sign that my life wasn't over; it was just beginning.

I stood and said to myself, *I'm taking my power back.* And for once, I meant it.

The Hartford Inn

By the time I finished packing my suitcase, I felt lighter than I had in years. My phone was still sitting face down on the counter. I half-expected Jeremy to call back, but thankfully, he didn't. The snow had thickened outside, blanketing Chicago in soft white silence. I stood at the window staring in awe of its beauty. I didn't feel dismissed or unheard; it was the beginning of a peaceful new start.

I loaded my luggage into the back of my SUV and took one last look at the house, our house. The one Jeremy tried to buy me out of. The place where we once dreamed, argued, and pretended that forever was possible. I exhaled slowly, locked the door, and whispered, "Goodbye."

The drive to Hartford, Connecticut, was long, almost twelve hours, but I didn't mind. I needed the distance; it was therapeutic. With every mile, the noise of my old life grew quieter. I listened to Christmas music to set the mood, stopped at random diners for coffee and desserts to keep me alert. I even smiled at a few cute guys along the way. It felt weird to be alone, but not in a bad way.

When I finally crossed into Hartford, it was late afternoon the next day. The town was alive with Christmas spirit unlike I've seen before. Twinkling lights strung across downtown streets, wreaths on every lamppost, and snow-dusted rooftops that looked like they were on a postcard. The scent of cinnamon and roasted nuts drifted from the bakeries and the outside Christmas vendors. I felt all warm inside and burst out laughing when I thought, *Jeremy, you can kick rocks with flip-flops.* I'd tucked away the prim, proper, professional attorney; I would be Jenny from the block for the next four weeks.

I pulled up in front of the Hartford Inn, a charming boutique hotel with brick walls, frosted windows, and a large wreath hanging on the front door. I had to pause; the Inn was so beautiful it stole a little breath right out of my chest. Tanya had reserved a suite for me overlooking the park. I could picture looking at the kids and their parents ice skating from my window, couples holding hands and children laughing as they slid on their bottoms across the ice.

As I checked in, the woman at the front desk welcomed me with a warm smile and greeting.

"Welcome to Hartford; you're just in time for our annual Christmas Festival. I believe you're going to enjoy your stay here."

I thanked her, took my room key card and rode the elevator up to my room. When I opened the door, I had to take a moment to let the Christmas beauty set in. The warmth of the Christmas figurines, along with a lush pine garland draped across the headboard and dotted with red berries, tiny ornaments, and shimmering ribbons, took my breath away.

The room was cozy with cream-colored walls, a fireplace flickering in the corner, and a beautiful window view just as I imagined. My phone vibrated and brought me back down to earth. It was my girl, Tanya.

"Girl, are you here yet? I'm bringing wine and peppermint bark. We're starting our celebration of your month-long Christmas vacation."

My voice, high with glee, blasted into the phone. "I just checked in," the words tumbled out, "and I'm ready for the festivities!"

When Tanya arrived twenty minutes later, she came in like a snowstorm; loud, dancing, laughing, and full of energy. Tanya was a twenty-nine-year-old melanated goddess, a little curvy, and full of life. Her hair fell naturally around her face, framing eyes that sparkled with mischief. She hugged me so tight that I swore my spine popped like bubble wrap.

"Girl, you look like you finally exhaled. I've been waiting for you to exhale. Now it's time to get your groove back," she said as she looked me square in the face and tossed my bangs to the side.

"Okay, now let's not get crazy on the first day," I said with pursed lips and furrowed eyebrows.

She opened the bottle of wine and told me to loosen up, then gave me a loving lecture.

"This trip isn't about Jeremy or Carol, or any of that mess and pettiness. It's about you finding peace, joy, and maybe some..." she grinned, and I shot her that look that I gave witnesses I was cross-examining.

"Jenny finding a little holiday magic is what I was going to say."

I laughed. "Yeah, right! That is absolutely not what you were going to say, ma'am. I think I've had enough so-called magic for a lifetime."

"Then it's time to get some of the right kind," she said.

She took her boots and socks off and flopped onto the hotel bed, patting the spot beside her. When I sat down, she grabbed the bottle of wine and glasses off the bedside table and poured us a full glass. We toasted to peace, to healing, and to whatever came next. For the first time in five years, I didn't feel bitter or broken over the betrayal by Jeremy and that home-wrecker Carol.

The Coffee Shop

Tanya and I spent the afternoon exploring Hartford. The city had a calm charm to it, quieter than the rustle and bustle of Chicago but full of life in its own way. Old brick buildings lined the streets, along with boutiques that had wreaths in their windows, and cafes with the smell of Christmas.

We stopped at a cozy spot called Bean & Brew, a local coffee shop Tanya swore served the best lattes in Connecticut. The moment I stepped into the quaint coffee shop, it felt like walking straight into one of those small-town Christmas movies everyone secretly wished were real. A tiny brass bell jingled over the door as we entered, and the spirit of the season hit me all at once, smelling of fresh-ground coffee, vanilla, and gingerbread.

Twinkling lights framed the windows, casting a soft glow on the snowflakes still melting on my coat. Red-and-green plaid runners adorned the wooden tables, and each held a small mason jar filled with holly and a flickering tea light, as if the town had decided that even the tiniest details deserved holiday magic.

A decorated Christmas tree stood proudly by the counter. Ornaments were a mix of handmade crafts from the local elementary school, crocheted snowflakes from the town library fundraiser, and a star on top that didn't quite sit straight, but somehow made it all feel even more charming.

A female barista wearing a Santa hat slightly too big for her head looked up with a soft, inviting expression that made me feel like I'd been coming there for years. Silent Night by The Temptations played in the background as milk steamed, laughter rang out, and two seniors played cards with what looked like peppermint mochas in hand.

It was simple, sweet, and just enough holiday joy to make me believe that this little town's Christmas miracles weren't just movie plots; they were entirely possible. And that's when I saw him. He stood behind the counter; a handsome Black man with warm brown skin and a smile that could melt snow. His build was lean but strong, like he'd probably played basketball. His short-cropped hair and trimmed beard framed his face perfectly. He looked up from the espresso machine just as I stepped forward, and for a split second, our eyes met.

He smiled. I looked away quickly, pretending to study the menu. Tanya nudged me.

"Girl, did you see how he looked at you? He's cute."

I shook my head. "Nope. Not doing this with you. I just got here, and you're trying to set me up. You're single; why don't you shoot your shot?"

"This isn't about me; it's about you. You don't have to worry about me. I get out, you don't. Do you even remember how to flirt?" She chuckled.

"Nope."

"You just need a little practice."

When I finally reached the counter, his eyes caught mine. "What can I get you?" he asked in a deep and smooth voice.

"Uh, just a caramel latte, please."

"Coming right up." He flashed a big warm smile. "This one's on the house. Do you live in Hartford? I never forget a beautiful face, and I haven't seen yours before."

"I'm visiting during the holidays. Thank you, but the free coffee isn't necessary."

"I insist."

I wanted to fight him on it but let it go.

"What's your name?" he asked with a grin. "I mean, I need it for your order."

"Jenny."

He slid the cup toward me a few minutes later. A little smiley face and my name were on it.

Tanya leaned in and whispered in my ear. "Oh, he's definitely flirting with you."

I laughed nervously. "He's just being nice."

"Nice? You're minimizing. Girl, he just gave you free coffee and wrote you a love emoji. That's flirting."

Before I could respond, he handed Tanya her drink and said, "Enjoy your latte. Maybe I'll see you two back here again tomorrow."

"Maybe you will," I said without meaning to.

As we walked back out into the cold, Tanya gave me a look that said everything. "You're in trouble."

The Christmas Market

That night, Tanya and I went to the Hartford outside Christmas Market. The square was lit up with Christmas lights and garlands showcasing the vendors. I was ready to tear up some roasted chestnuts, hot chocolate, and snickerdoodle cookies. It felt like stepping into a Hallmark Christmas movie.

Tanya linked her arm through mine as we walked past the vendors and food trucks. "See? Isn't this better than sitting in a hotel room?"

I forced a smile. "I'll admit, this is nice. And yes, it's better than chilling in my room."

"Now that's the spirit," she grinned and blew me a kiss.

We stopped at a booth selling handmade ornaments when I heard a familiar voice behind me.

"Well, if it isn't my favorite coffee shop customer."

I turned around, and there he was — the cute barista. I had to admit he looked even more handsome than he had earlier today. He wore a black pea coat with a dark red scarf and a matching hat.

"Hey there," I said, taken aback in the best way.

"Jenny..." he drawled with that handsome smile and cute dimples. "By the way, my name is Marcus. I'm volunteering here tonight. Helping with the toy drive booth just down the row."

"I know your name from your employee's name tag," I quipped, then hoped I didn't appear rude. To save face, I continued. "It's great that you're taking time to volunteer." My tone and expression softened as I was genuinely impressed with him. "Do you volunteer a lot in the community?"

He shrugged modestly. "I try. My parents raised me to give back whenever I have an opportunity. My mother runs a bakery close to here, so she donates treats and sponsors the toy drive every year."

"Small world," I chuckled. "Tanya and I were just talking about volunteering somewhere while we're here."

He glanced over his shoulder. "Then come join me, ladies," he suggested, his voice echoing slightly in the crisp air. "We could always use an extra pair of hands."

Tanya was already nodding before I could think about it. "We'd love to," she squealed.

An hour later, we were standing beside Marcus volunteering. All three of us wore Santa hats under a tent filled with wrapped toys and boxes of donated clothes. He had an easy, gentle manner with the kids who came by; warm, patient, always smiling. Watching him joke with a little girl about which doll she should pick out made my heart flutter.

When the crowd slowed down, he turned to me. "You're a natural at this."

I laughed. "I'm a lawyer. My job's arguing for a living. It felt good to put a smile on the cute little faces of the children."

He stepped a little closer. "I can tell you've got a kind heart." A warm smile spread across his face, showcasing his dimples and softening the corners of his eyes.

My heart fluttered, but my phone rang before I could respond. It was an associate from my firm. I stepped away to take the call.

"Hey, Tara, what's going on?"

The junior associate was nervous as ever. "Hi, I was reviewing the Harris' file, and I noticed there's a discrepancy between the client's statement and the police report. Do you know whether we verified which version is accurate?"

"Yes, the client's statement was updated after our follow-up interview. Make sure you're referencing the most recent version."

I listened patiently to her response before saying, "You didn't need to call me for this. You could've figured that out yourself. If you want to move up, you've got to trust your own instincts, okay? I will not be available to make time for every little question."

She apologized immediately, and I softened my tone. "Don't be sorry. You've got this, and I trust you. You need to trust yourself."

After hanging up, I turned back to Marcus, who was watching me with a curious smile.

"Work stuff?"

"Yeah," I said with a sigh. "Even on vacation, they find me."

He chuckled. "That's what happens when you're the boss."

"Apparently."

We finished our shift laughing. Tanya had walked away, giving us time to talk. He was so charming and intelligent. It made me wonder why he was a barista. Not in a job-shaming way, just that I could see him in the professional arena. We walked back to the table and packed up the last few boxes. Then, Marcus turned to me.

"I'm glad you came tonight," he said with a twinkle in his eyes.

"Me too," I admitted.

And when he smiled at me again, I suddenly realized that I wasn't thinking about Jeremy and Carol, the "marriage burglar." My mind was on getting to know this kind man. It didn't hurt that he was fine to boot.

Christmas Pies

The next afternoon, I drove over to Tanya's parents' house. As I crossed the threshold, I smelled something sweet coming from the kitchen. With all the decorations and arrangements, the Daniels' house had a festive vibe. It was a gray brick house with green shutters, a pleasant feature to enhance the home. There were wreaths in the windows. A light dusting of snow covered the porch steps.

When I rang the bell, Tanya flung the door open wearing an oversized sweatshirt that said, "Bakers Gonna Bake."

"Finally!" she said, pulling me inside. "I thought you would never get here."

"Now you know I wouldn't miss this." I laughed. "I stopped for more flour because your mom apparently has a pie factory going on in here and sent me a text to pick up two pounds of flour."

I heard her mother call out from the kitchen, "I heard that, Jenny! Now come on in here and help before this crust gets tough!"

"Yes, ma'am." I smiled and tilted my head at Tanya. "Told ya."

The kitchen was alive with music from the Braxton's Mary Did You Know Christmas hit. Tanya's father sat at the table tapping his foot, pretending to be tired of the Christmas tradition. Pie ingredients, rolling pins, and measuring cups covered the counters.

Mrs. Daniels looked up from the counter, her apron dusted with flour. "We're making sweet potato, pecan, and apple pies," she said proudly. "We freeze them now so they'll taste perfect on Christmas Eve."

Tanya handed me a rolling pin. "Come on, partner. Let's get to work."

For the next hour, the three of us rolled, mixed, and laughed while the music played. Tanya teased her dad for sneaking bites of pie filling, and he defended himself like he was on trial. I couldn't remember the last time I'd laughed so hard. Probably not since before everything with Jeremy. When we finally took a break, Mrs. Daniels poured us mugs of hot chocolate made with real milk and topped with a mountain of whipped cream.

Mrs. Daniel looked over at me. "Tanya tells us you've been experiencing some tough times lately with Jeremy remarrying."

My face fell, and my mood dampened. I tried not to cry, but I couldn't stop the river of tears. "Mrs. Daniels, it was too much for me. Everything from divorce to business-related problems. I honestly don't know why Carol, the wrecking ball, and Jeremy, the side-piece snatcher, hooked up in the first place. We were happy, and the firm was thriving. He was my person, you know? MY person, not hers!" I choked out as I wiped the back of my hand across my wet cheeks. "He kissed me every morning and held me every night after making love. Our marriage was perfect."

Jenny slid a tissue into my hand, her face soft with worry. "Girl, that man fooled all of us. I had never seen you two argue, and he acted like you hung the moon," she whispered. Tanya stepped in behind me, wrapping her arms around my shoulders in one of those grounding hugs. "So, when we heard about that affair, especially with Carol of all people—we were all stunned," she murmured as I sat there at the table, tears spilling, both of them comforting me the best they could.

Mrs. Daniels reached out and gently took my hand in hers, her eyes soft with empathy.

"Oh, Jenny... I can't pretend to know exactly how you feel, but I know this: you loved Jeremy, and you did your best in the marriage. That says more about you than any betrayal ever could. Pain like this doesn't define you; it just shows how brave and resilient you are for opening your heart to love. One day, you'll look back and see that what you built for yourself is stronger than anything anyone else could take away."

I squeezed her hand so tight.

"Thank you. I needed to be here tonight. I've spent the last five years trying to hold it all together, and honestly, I'm just tired. Coming to Hartford provided the getaway I needed from everything and just breathe."

A soft smile graced Mrs. Daniels' face. "Peace doesn't come from holding on to the past, honey. It comes from letting go."

The words she said resonated with me on a profound level.

"That's what I'm learning. Thank you all for making me feel at home. I love you both dearly." Mr. Daniels felt excluded. He tapped the kitchen table to get our attention and cupped his fingers together, forming a perfect heart.

Tanya leaned her chin on my head and tickled my sides. "We love you, too, and you know that you're family. I love seeing you here, laughing again and baking and eating pie with me, Mama and Daddy. That's healing, Jen."

"If healing tastes like this pie, I'll take it." I laughed.

Her dad chuckled and raised his mug. "To healing and my girls."

This Christmas by Chris Brown came on, and Tanya grabbed my hand and pulled me to the center of the kitchen.

"Come on, dance with me! You know this is one of your favorite songs and Christmas movies."

At first, I protested, but within seconds, I was swaying with her, laughing, and moving to the smooth rhythm. It was wonderful, and the Christmas spirit filled my heart. Later that night, when the pies were cooling, and the snow fell heavier outside, Tanya and I sat on her parents' porch wrapped in blankets.

"You know," she said, "I saw how Marcus looked at you at the toy drive yesterday."

"Don't start." I rolled my eyes playfully.

She started grinning and shaking her head. "I'm just saying, girl, he's fine, and he's clearly interested in you. You deserve someone like Marcus."

I stared into the distance for a second. "I don't know if I'm ready for that again. We did exchange numbers last night."

"And you're just now telling me this?" Tanya asked, her eyebrows shooting up and her hand flying to her mouth as she leaned back a little, like my words had physically knocked her off balance.

"You're not getting it." I said with a little frustration in my voice. "I don't think I'm ready," I whispered, pulling my coat tighter around me as snowflakes landed on my hair and melted against my face.

My hands trembled in my lap, and I pulled my arms across my chest, trying to keep the ache from spilling over. "I'm afraid of being hurt again. Jeremy's affair tore me apart. It wasn't just a betrayal; it was like this frigid wind we're feeling now cutting through me back then like shard glass. It settled in my chest and froze every part of me that trusted him. Every memory of him with Carol haunted me for years. How am I supposed to risk all that again?"

"It may not be all about being ready, sweetie," Tanya said. "Maybe it's about being open to the idea in the future."

Tanya leaned closer and brushed a snowflake off my shoulder.

"Jenny," she whispered, "you've survived something that could have broken anyone. I'm not sure I could have shown such grace in the midst of the turmoil. It's okay to move slowly, but you have to move. You don't owe your heart to anyone until you're ready. One day, someone will see all the pieces you've protected and love them without hurting you. That's kinda what my mom was telling you tonight. But hey, for now ... just live life. Feel the cold, let it remind you that you're still alive and that's enough, okay?"

I was speechless - she was right. Right then, I saw Marcus' face in my mind; I heard his boisterous laugh echoing in the atmosphere. I was still thinking about his smile and those big brown eyes. I should open myself up to meeting new people and making a genuine connection.

The Date

Marcus called the next morning while I was sipping coffee in my hotel room and thinking about him. I nearly spilled my drink with the excitement of hearing his voice; excitement that surprised me.

"Good morning, Jenny," he said. "I hope I didn't wake you."

I blushed. "No, I was just deciding whether to get dressed or stay in my pajamas all day. I haven't decided yet."

"Well, if you're not too busy doing that, I'd love to take you to dinner tonight. There's a small restaurant on the riverfront that plays live jazz on Fridays. I think you'd like it."

My heart raced. "That sounds ... nice."

"Great. I'll pick you up at 7:00 p.m. Is that time good for you?"

"Seven it is." Excitement rippled through me, and I did a little shimmy I couldn't quite contain.

When I hung up, I sat there staring at my reflection in the hotel mirror. My hair was a mess, I had no makeup on, and I looked nothing like someone a man like Marcus would take out. I got out of bed and walked to the hair salon down the street. I didn't want to drive because walking allowed me to feel the cold air on my face, and I could enjoy the beautiful scenery.

All day, I tried to focus on other things, but my mind kept drifting to my dinner date with Marcus. By the time I started getting ready, my nerves were already doing cartwheels. I slipped into a black wrap dress, simple but elegant, and added a hint of red lipstick Tanya had sworn would accentuate my skin tone.

When Marcus arrived, the sight of him literally took my breath away. He stood at my door in a charcoal suit; his coat brushed with a few snowflakes. He smiled at me and extended his hand for mine, kissing it. It was such a gentle, romantic gesture.

"Wow," he said, his eyebrows lifted, softening his face as he took my arm and turned me around until the sight of my outfit stole his breath. "You look beautiful, Jenny."

I looked him up and down with an impressed smile. "Thank you. You clean up pretty well yourself."

He laughed and offered his arm. "Shall we?"

The drive to the restaurant was wonderful. Marcus told me more about the Christmas traditions here, the glitter of lights on every lamppost, and why the city looked like it was dipped in gold. The Harborlight restaurant sat right by the river, its windows glowing with soft amber light. Inside, a jazz trio played a smooth rendition of The Christmas Song.

We sat by the window, and the frozen water outside reflected the magnificent lights. For a while, we just talked, easing into each other's company.

"What's your favorite Christmas movie?" he asked, leaning back slightly in his chair.

His dimples mesmerized me. "Oh, that's easy, but I have two. They both tie for the number one spot." I laughed.

"This Christmas and It's a Wonderful Life. I've watched them at least ten times every holiday," I said with a grin. "What's yours? And don't tell me Die Hard."

"Elf,' hands down," he replied, chuckling. "I mean, come on, Buddy the Elf? Classic. But Die Hard comes in as a solid second. Come on, Bruce Willis!"

"I should have guessed that. You seem like a Buddy the Elf type," I laughed.

"I'll take that as a compliment." He smirked. "What about traditions? Any family rituals for the holidays?"

I thought for a moment. "Well, my family always decorates the tree together, and we bake cookies—lots, and lots of cookies. This is my first year away from home for the holidays. I needed something different this year; my parents supported my coming to Hartford. What about you?"

He leaned forward, eyes lit up. "I used to help my mom at her bakery when I was a teenager after my dad passed unexpectedly from congestive heart failure. It was just us. I would steal frosting from the freshly baked cookies and cakes. I was a little scamp, and it drove my mom crazy. My mother always made Christmas special for me. I used to find my gifts before Christmas. I even tried on the clothes. My mom would hide them in the same place every year, the back of her closet. I would act so surprised every year when opening the gifts. My mother was in pure bliss seeing my joy at Christmas. I forgot about this. Don't laugh too hard. There was a gift wrapped with my name on it; I carefully opened it up, and it was an older man's sweater. The gift was for my uncle, whom I'm named after. You should have seen me trying to wrap it back up the way my mom had it!"

I laughed so hard at his stories and wiped tears from my eyes. "You were a little troublemaker, huh?"

"Maybe a little," he admitted with a laugh. "But it was fun. Those were some of the best memories with my mom."

"Ohh, I love that," I said softly, listening attentively to his every word. "It's nice to hear about family memories that are happy, even with the hard stuff mixed in."

He nodded and shifted his posture, glancing out the window for a second, then back at me. "Yeah. They stick with you. I guess that's why holidays always feel special, no matter what's going on."

I smiled. "You're a good son. It's obvious you're a tremendous help to your mother and her bakery."

He smiled back. "I'm trying to. Mom still runs circles around me in the kitchen, though. I mostly handle the business side of things, you know, contracts, suppliers, marketing. The less I'm near the frosting now, the better."

"So, you're a barista and a businessman? You're handling the financials and other parts of the family business," I said, as I tilted my head, feeling moved and smitten.

"Something like that," he said, his eyes locked with mine. "And you're an attorney who looks like she belongs in the city lights of Hartford with a handsome barista."

I didn't know how to respond to that. The compliment sat a little heavy in my chest. After dinner, we shared a rich chocolate mousse with peppermint cream for dessert. I didn't even want dessert, but when he offered me a bite from his spoon, I couldn't resist. The taste, the music, the way he looked at me; it all felt like something out of a dream I didn't know I wanted until I came to Hartford.

As we left the restaurant, snow began to fall again. Marcus reached for my hand as we walked toward the car.

"Are you okay? You've seemed to have shut down," he asked with visible creases in his forehead.

"Yes," I said, looking up at the snowflakes. "Just taking it all in. It's been a long time since I've felt this happy."

He squeezed my hand gently. "Then I'm glad I asked you to dinner."

When he dropped me off at the hotel, he didn't rush to leave. We talked in the lobby for a while. He turned toward me with those warm eyes and said, "I had a wonderful time with you tonight, Jenny."

"Me too," I whispered while looking into his eyes that I got lost in for a minute.

He smiled and stepped closer to me but not close enough to kiss me.

"Goodnight." He walked away, his cologne leaving me standing there with my heart pounding and my cheeks flushed.

That night, I couldn't sleep. Every time I closed my eyes, I replayed in my mind his smile, those dimples, his smooth and sexy voice, and the way he looked at me like Jeremy used to before Carol the man snatcher sunk her claws into him.

Art and Pastries

The morning after our date, I marveled at how lovely it went, except I was salty because he didn't kiss me. Holding a mug of hot chocolate brimming with marshmallows, I stood at my hotel window. Below, bundled in scarves and boots, people hurried past, laden with shopping bags and steaming drinks. I was in heaven.

Tanya called around 9:00 a.m. "It's time for you to get dressed, girl. We're going shopping before you hide in that room all day thinking about that date you need to tell me all about."

"Shopping? I thought we were taking it easy today."

"We are; easy means hitting the Christmas market, grabbing lunch, and maybe stopping by the coffee shop and saying hi to your boyfriend."

I shook my head and smiled. "You really don't quit, do you? But take me to the museum today. I think I've shopped enough."

"The museum sounds good, and no, I don't quit when I'm seeing that spark in you again."

***

The outside of the museum had me hooked as soon as we got there. There were Christmas angels and a beautiful Christmas train where you could sit and take pictures. When I entered the museum, the cold trailed in behind me, clinging to my coat before the warmth eased into my skin. Evergreen ropes lined the banisters, dressed in soft white lights that glimmered like tiny winter stars. The air held a scent of cinnamon and pecans, like holiday memories had been simmering somewhere out of sight.

People strolled through the halls, their shoes barely making a sound on the shiny floors, which echoed softly up to the high ceilings. People were laughing and chatting quietly, and the choir's carols echoed through the museum, sounding heavenly, like the Mormon Tabernacle Choir.

The exhibits were all adorned with seasonal touches: wreaths framed the artwork, sparkling ornaments graced glass displays, and a towering, shimmering Christmas tree dominated the atrium. I stood still, my breath hitched as I took it all in. It wasn't just festive; it was enchanting. I'd literally stepped into a living holiday story.

"I had such a good time with Marcus last night," I said as Tanya and I walked past a giant Christmas train covered in antique glass ornaments. "Like ... I'm still smiling about it."

Tanya narrowed her eyes like she had questions. "Mmhmm. So why does your voice sound all disappointed?"

"Because he didn't kiss me goodnight. I felt the chemistry, and based on the evidence, his tone, body language, the way he kept looking at me, and I swear he was mapping my lips. I'm about ninety-nine percent certain the chemistry was mutual." I sighed like an attorney who had just lost an appeal.

She stopped in front of a display of vintage Christmas cards and turned to me slowly. "Wait! What? No kiss, not even on the cheek?"

"Nothing," I said, shaking my head. "Just a hug. I mean, it was a long and tight hug, but still a doggone hug."

Tanya scoffed. "Girl, please. Men act shy when they are actually feeling you. He probably didn't wanna mess it up."

"I don't know," I said, staring at a carousel of tiny toy sleighs. "It felt like the perfect moment."

She gave me that "don't play with me look. "Okay, so we need to do something about this."

"Oh Lord..." I muttered. "Here you go."

"Don't 'here you go' me," she said, as she playfully pushed me toward a hallway lined with life-sized nutcrackers. "We're going to Sweet Grace Bakery."

I stopped walking. "His mama's bakery? Tanya, I know you're not serious."

"I'm serious as a heart attack, and we're going today," she said, picking up a program from a table shaped like a snowflake. "If you wanna know about a man, meet the woman who raised him."

"We just went on one date," I reminded her.

"And you said it was a great date," she said with base in her voice. "Plus, his mama raised him. She's probably why he's out here acting all gentlemanly instead of making a move."

I stared at her. "You're a trip."

"You know I'm right," she said, looking at the time on her phone. "Come on. We'll swing by the bakery. His mama might need some customers from Chicago."

I shook my head, laughing. "Girl…"

"Trust me," Tanya said, pointing at the gingerbread village like it held ancient wisdom. "His mama is the key." She drove me to Sweet Grace Bakery, and when we arrived, I opened the door to see…

"Gezzus, Tanya, look, there he is! Why isn't he working at the coffee shop? Let's go!" I said as I pushed past Tanya.

"No, ma'am," she pushed back. "It's too late; he has already spotted us."

Marcus stood behind the counter, helping his mom box up pastries for a line of customers. His eyes lit up when he waved us in. Butterflies swarmed in my belly like he was my first crush or something.

"He's sooo fine, and that sweater is doing things for him."

"Stop," I whispered, trying to hide my glee at seeing him.

"Fine," she whispered back, "but you better take your happy tail up to that counter and talk to him and his mother."

I promised I would, even though I wasn't sure why she wanted me to do this, but I really wanted to get to see where things could go with him.

"Hi, Marcus! I didn't know you would be here. I came to buy some of your mother's pastries."

"I'm glad you stopped by and I was here." He turned around and said, "Look, Mom, Jenny, and her friend, Tanya, are here."

"Oh, hello ladies. Jenny, my son has been talking about you all morning." She gave him a wink.

I couldn't believe what she had just said. He'd been thinking of me, too.

"He's a charmer, but I'm pretty sure you know that," I replied with a smile stretching from ear to ear.

The bakery was swamped, so I didn't want to keep them. Tanya and I bought several goodies as we were leaving. Marcus shouted goodbye and told me he would call me later.

CHRISTMAS IN HARTFORD

I was in trouble. This man had me falling for him for real-for real.

The Christmas Mixer

The next night, I was dressing for Marcus' mother's Christmas mixer. He asked me to stop by when he called. We were on the phone until the wee hours of the morning. I told him how my parents had worked hard to send me to college and law school. He told me about graduating with his master's in business administration. I knew that man belonged in the professional arena. He made me want to stay in Hartford, to be near him.

An hour later, Tanya and I made our way to Sweet Grace Bakery. As soon as we stepped inside, live elves and Santa greeted us at the door with candy canes. Grace, Marcus's mother, spotted us first.

"Jenny, sweetheart, come in! Tanya, welcome!"

She looked radiant, with silver curls pinned up and a red apron tied neatly around her waist. "You must try one of my peppermint brownies before Marcus eats the rest."

I took a napkin and got two brownies. "Yes, ma'am, I've heard rumors about these."

I took a bite. The brownies melted in my mouth. They tasted like chocolate luxury, warm, chewy, and not too sweet.

"Umm...Ms. Grace, the rumors are true." I smiled and gave her a side hug.

"I'm so glad you liked them. You must come by the bakery more while you're here."

Then I saw Marcus, looking as handsome as ever. He was standing near the back, talking to a volunteer, wearing a dark green sweater that made him look even more irresistible. The second he saw me, his expression turned soft enough to make my knees wobble.

"You came," he said, leaving the person he was talking to and walking toward me.

"I told you we would."

He leaned in to hug me, his voice a low rumble. "And I told you I was hoping you would."

We talked near the apple cider and cookie table while Tanya disappeared to mingle. He poured me a cup of cider. "Careful," he said softly, "it's hot."

"You always bring me something sweet," I teased.

"What can I say?" he smiled. "I'm a believer in giving sweetness to the sweet."

As soon as we finished our drinks, Marcus set them down and then grabbed my hand, pulling me toward the dance floor.

"Marcus!" I squeaked, but I couldn't help following his lead.

We danced to the Christmas songs, and as we swayed, he spun me in a slow circle and dipped me like we were in one of those old black-and-white movies.

It felt so natural I never wanted to let go. Marcus' voice interrupted my thoughts as he murmured in my ear, our bodies still swaying to the beat. "Hartford's got this heartbeat I never tire of. Our intimate cafés on every corner, and people who'll talk to you like they've known you forever."

The more he whispered in my ear, the more I felt myself falling for him.

When he told me about his mentoring program for kids, I couldn't help but wish he lived closer to me.

"You're really something, Marcus Porter," I murmured, the awe in my voice impossible to hide.

"Just trying to give back." He took my hand.

I looked up and noticed the mistletoe hanging above us.

"Would you look at that?" I said, pointing above our heads.

Marcus followed my gaze, then looked back at me with a grin. "Guess it's Christmas law."

Before I knew it, my body reacted, and I kissed him. His lips were soft and coaxed mine for more. The room shrank around us, as if we were the only ones there. He pulled me close to him and wrapped his arms around my waist. My entire body relaxed, and I felt safe in his arms. When he finally pulled back, his forehead brushed mine, his voice low and full of wonder, he whispered, "For me, this counts as my Christmas miracle."

"Me too," I said as I grabbed the back of his head and went full throttle kissing him this time.

He lifted my chin and looked into my eyes. "I think this is one of the greatest Christmases I've ever had."

I melted like butter and repeated my previous words. "Me too."

More Pies

That night I lay in bed thinking about him. I had forgotten that Tanya had invited me to her parents' house tomorrow for yet another pie-baking marathon. This time it was for charity. Proceeds would benefit a local after-school program. I turned on some Christmas movies, texted my parents, and went to sleep.

When I arrived at Tanya's mom's the next morning, Mrs. Daniels was in full throttle; rolling out crusts on the counter like someone on the Food Network. She would hum to herself as she cooked whenever she made those special dishes for her loved ones. I'd noticed that about her. Mrs. Daniels loved helping others, but she carried a subtle fear that nothing she did was ever enough, that the kids, the family, even Tanya, deserved better than she could give.

Despite that, she had an abundance of love that filled a room. She'd paused mid-roll when she saw me, giving me a crooked smile, as if she and I had a private joke. I laughed and pressed my hand to my heart. I realized again why Tanya loved having me over here. She could see how her mother always lifted my spirits.

Mrs. Daniels threw a towel at her husband. "Turn my song up," she said with a grin.

Her father, Mr. Daniels, sat at the table, tapping his foot to The Temptations' Silent Night. "Okay, dear."

"Jenny, sweetheart, grab an apron," Mrs. Daniels said as she fiercely kneaded that dough. "We're making French silk pies this year. Get over here; I don't allow slackers in this kitchen."

"Yes, ma'am." I laughed as I tied the apron on.

For the next hour, we rolled dough, told stories, and laughed until our stomachs hurt. It was loud, messy, and wonderful.

At one point, Mrs. Daniels looked up at me. "Tanya tells us you've been seeing that nice young man from the coffee shop."

CHRISTMAS IN HARTFORD

I nodded slowly and gave Tanya a look for spilling the beans. "We're getting to know each other. He seems to be a genuine person."

Mrs. Daniels smiled. "You deserve all the happiness life has to give you. Don't ever forget that, honey." Her words hit me like a hard truth I hadn't wanted to admit until now.

Later, when "Silent Night" came back on, Mr. Daniels turned the volume up and said, "Can't bake without The Temptations."

He grabbed his wife and danced like there was a dance floor in the kitchen with that disco ball hovering over them.

Tanya and I went upstairs to her room. "So ... what's crack-a-lacking with you and Marcus?"

"Girl, I'm not ready to go back to my life in Chicago. There's no stress here and..."

"You want to see where things could go with Marcus, don't you?" She abruptly cut me off while I was still in the middle of speaking.

"Okay, girl, you win, yes!" I said loud and proud with a huge grin that told everything.

The Surprise

The next morning, I lay in bed reading "Christmas in Crestview" by Latoya Geter. It was a sweet read. I recommended it to Tanya. When I finished the book and wrote my five-star review on Amazon and Goodreads, I opened my curtains, and the sunlight spilled in through the hotel window, showcasing the snowflakes drifting lazily outside. It was almost Christmas Eve.

Tanya called to check in before heading to the square. "You sure you don't want to come sing carols with us?"

I smiled, stretching by the window. "I'll leave that to the professionals. Besides, I think my contribution to Christmas spirit will be binge-watching old holiday movies today."

She laughed. "Suit yourself. Just don't watch It's a Wonderful Life without me."

"Never."

After we hung up, I brewed some coffee and pulled on my favorite sweatshirt. I spent the morning watching Home Alone, mouthing the lines like I had when I was a kid. Marcus crossed my mind several times.

Around 9:00 a.m., there was a knock at the door. I opened it to find one of the hotel staff holding a large box wrapped in shiny red and gold paper.

"Ms. Thompson?"

"That's me," I said.

"This package was dropped off for you earlier this morning. The sender didn't leave a name."

"Really? No card?" I blinked several times.

He shook his head. "Just said to make sure it was delivered at nine sharp."

I thanked him, handed him a tip, and closed the door. For a moment I just stood there staring at the gift, excited to see what it was and who had sent it to me.

Curiosity got the best of me. I tore off the wrapping carefully and lifted the lid. Inside was the most beautiful dress I'd ever seen; a deep, rich Christmas red with soft satin that shimmered under the light. It was elegant and breathtaking.

There was a folded note nestled inside the box.

Jenny, I have a gala tonight, and I'd be honored if you'd come as my guest.

Black tie, Christmas spirit, and hopefully a little magic.

Warm wishes,

Marcus

The scream I let out from Marcus' gift and invitation. My body tingled as I picked up my phone and called him.

When he answered, his voice was warm and teasing. "So, did Santa find your hotel room?" He chuckled.

"Yes!" I laughed. "Marcus, this dress is beautiful. I can't believe you did this. Of course, I'll go with you! Yes, yes, yes!"

He chuckled. "I was hoping you'd say that. I'll pick you up at 7:00 p.m."

When we ended the call, I held the dress up against me in the mirror. It was perfect. The fit, the color — everything. For a few seconds, I just stared at my reflection, smiling like a woman who finally believed in Christmas magic again.

The Gala

By the time 7:00 p.m. rolled around, I was ready and excited to see Marcus dressed in his suit. My hair was in soft curls around my shoulders, and the red dress flowed like liquid silk when I moved. My heels clicked softly on the floor as I paced the room waiting for him to pick me up.

When the knock came, I took a deep breath before opening the door. And there he was, looking like he had just stepped out of a GQ magazine. Marcus looked incredible in his black suit that was perfectly tailored, crisp white shirt, dark tie, and that cologne I loved smelling on him.

His eyes widened when he saw me. "Wow, Jenny. You look... stunning."

I felt my cheeks warm. "Thank you. You look pretty sharp yourself."

He laughed softly and stepped inside, holding my coat — a long cream-colored winter coat lined with faux fur at the collar. He lifted it carefully and draped it around my shoulders. "Please allow me."

When his fingers brushed the back of my neck, I shivered, and it wasn't from the cold.

"Thank you," I said, turning to face him.

He smiled, his eyes kind. "You're welcome. You deserve to be treated like this. Jenny, you're special, and don't forget it."

I kissed him gently on the cheek. He smiled. "I look forward to getting more of those."

We both laughed, and he offered his arm. "Shall we?"

As we stepped into the hotel lobby, I caught sight of the limousine waiting outside. "Oh, somebody has limousine service tonight?"

He grinned. "You do."

"Wait—this is for us?"

"Yes," he said simply. "I wanted this night to be special for you. You deserve it, don't you think?"

How could he afford this? "Awww ... Marcus. I love this. No one's ever done anything like this for me before."

"Then it's about time," he said, opening the door for me.

The limo was softly lit, with a bottle of champagne chilling next to chocolate-covered strawberries. I laughed softly. "You really thought of everything."

"I just wanted to see you smile like that," he said with a grin.

We clinked glasses, sipped champagne as the city lights blurred by outside the windows. My heart finally felt like it was ready to trust again.

When we arrived at the gala, the grandeur took my breath away. Marble floors gleamed beneath crystal chandeliers, and people in elegant attire mingled, their laughter echoing through the ballroom.

Marcus greeted everyone with easy charm, introducing me to business owners, local officials, and familiar faces from around Hartford. I smiled and shook hands, pretending not to be surprised that a barista seemed to know half the city's elite.

Then it hit me; it was his mother's bakery. Sweet Grace wasn't just popular; she was legendary in Hartford. Of course, he'd grown up surrounded by half of these people.

As we walked toward the bar for a glass of wine, I spotted a familiar face: Tanya. She looked radiant in a sleek emerald dress, her arm looped through the arm of a handsome man I didn't recognize. When she and I ended up next to each other at the bar, I nudged her playfully. "Okay, you came here with a mystery man and didn't even tell me. Spill it."

She laughed. "I was waiting to see how long it would take you to ask. His name's Greg, my old boyfriend from the eleventh grade."

My eyes widened. "Wait, that Greg?"

She nodded. "Yep. My mom called his mom, don't ask — and apparently, they decided we needed to 'catch up.' We started talking again, and, I don't know, Jenny. There's something there."

I smiled, delighted. "So you're telling me you're circling the block back to your high school sweetheart?"

She laughed. "You know I don't circle the block. But he said if things go well, he'd move to Chicago. His job's remote."

"Now that's a Christmas reunion I like, Tanya."

We toasted with our drinks before heading back to our dates, smiling like two women who might be falling in love during the holidays.

Falling Hard

The gala wrapped up just after midnight. Marcus and I stepped out of the ballroom hand in hand. The limousine sat quietly at the curb, but Marcus's eyes caught a horse-drawn carriage, its lanterns casting a warm glow over the fresh snow.

He led me across the street, my heels crunching on top of the snow. The horse's breath came in gentle clouds, steam rising from its nostrils in the frosty night. The driver, an older man in a thick coat and wool cap, tipped his hat as Marcus opened the carriage door for me. "Good evening, the ride is free tonight. Hop on in and enjoy the ride," he said, his voice gentle and kind.

I slid in, and Marcus followed, tucking the blanket around us. The horse trotted, its hooves tapping a steady rhythm on the cobblestone and snow, a soft jingle echoed in the night. The white falling snow caught the light like glitter—and all I could feel was the warmth of Marcus next to me.

His warm breath was on my face. His arms draped around my shoulders, and I leaned into him, resting my head lightly on his chest. I could feel the steady beat of his heart through the fabric of his coat, a rhythm that somehow matched the trot of the horse. Every time he shifted closer, every brush of his fingers against mine, made my chest tighten, made me forget the city, the cold, even myself.

Across the street, I spotted Tanya and Greg climbing into their car. Tanya's face lit up, and she waved like a madwoman.

"Okay, I see you two lovebirds!" Her laughter rang through the snow.

I giggled, pressing my hand over my mouth. "Good night, you two. I'll call you later, Tanya."

Marcus's laughter at Tanya rumbled softly in the carriage. He leaned over and gave me a soft kiss on my temple; this man sent shivers down my spine.

The horse carried us several blocks. I wanted it to last forever. The horse jerked a bit, and I placed my head back on his chest. I felt safe, cared for, and I realized, fully and irrevocably, that I was falling in love with him.

And just like that, the ride had come to an end. We thanked the driver, and Marcus gave him a $100 tip. I hoped that didn't set him back. We climbed into the limousine. I leaned back in my seat as the city lights flickered by, still replaying the night in my head. The music, his holding me tight as we danced, the laughter, and his showing me it was okay to let my guard down.

When we pulled up to the hotel, Marcus got out first and offered me his hand. I took it, stepping down carefully in my high heels, but still lost my balance. Inside the lobby, everything was quiet; only the desk clerk was in there.

"I had an amazing time tonight," I said as I pulled him in to hold me once more.

He smiled and held me tight for like a minute. "So did I; you made the night a Christmas dream."

"Thank you for everything," I said softly as I looked into his big brown eyes. "The dress, the limo, the dinner — everything was perfect. I would love for you to be my date at Tanya's family's house tomorrow for the Christmas Eve festivities."

He gazed into my eyes and lifted my chin, voice low and sincere. "I wanted to give you a night you'd remember. You deserve that, Jenny. And, yes, I would love to spend Christmas Eve with you in any capacity."

He kissed me before I could respond. The kiss was deeper this time; he was falling for me as hard as I was falling for him. It felt dangerously close to love.

When we finally pulled apart, I smiled, my heart pounding. "I'd better go up to my room. Goodnight, Marcus."

With a warm tone, he said, "Goodnight, Jenny. Sleep well; I'll see you soon in my dreams."

My heart fluttered so hard it almost hurt. I bit my lip, trying to play it cool, but inside, I was melting. He had no idea what he was doing to me. As he turned to leave, I watched him go, my heart full in a way it hadn't been for years. I walked into the elevator, and when the elevator doors closed behind me, I whispered to myself, "He's the one. I'm finally ready."

Christmas Eve

Christmas Eve at Tanya's parents' house was nothing short of enchanting. As soon as Marcus and I entered with our Christmas gifts, we were greeted with hugs. They took the gifts and placed them under the tree. I bought Marcus a gift earlier today. I was surprised when he picked me up and he had gifts for me and Tanya's family. The Christmas tree had more decorations than yesterday.

It stood tall in the living room, with icicles, family photos, and a glowing Black Angel at the top. They had removed the star. The scent of chocolate chip cookies, turkey, and ham filled the air. The stockings hung perfectly over the fireplace, and Nat King Cole played in the background.

Tanya's mom told us to make ourselves at home. Greg, Tanya's boyfriend, was already there, helping her dad carry a few extra chairs into the dining room. Tanya looked so happy. Seeing her and Greg together, laughing and moving around each other so naturally, made my night.

Marcus was wearing a cozy ugly Christmas sweater. Tanya's dad, Greg, and uncle immediately took him under their wings, pulling him into the living room to talk sports, laugh loudly, and pretend they weren't all sneaking the cookies that were cooling on the counter.

Meanwhile, Tanya, her mother, and I were in the kitchen preparing dishes for Christmas Eve dinner. The kitchen smelled heavenly with sweet potatoes, collard greens, and turkey seasoning; it was the essence of the holidays.

But of course, it wouldn't be Christmas without Tanya and her mom having one of their little debates.

"Tanya, why are you using margarine?" Her mother scolded, hands on her hips.

"Because it's what was in the fridge, Mama," Tanya said, rolling her eyes but trying to hide a grin.

Her mother pointed toward the refrigerator. "That's not how we make homemade mashed potatoes. We use butter. Butter gives it soul."

Tanya huffed dramatically, putting the margarine back and pulling out the butter. "Fine! Butter it is. But if this butter makes these potatoes too rich, you're eating them all yourself."

Her mom laughed. "Girl, you'll be lucky if there's any left to eat after your daddy gets a hold of them."

We all burst into laughter, and I couldn't help but think how much I loved moments like this; the sound of family teasing, the feeling of togetherness, the smell of food cooking and memories being made.

Later that night, we gathered in the living room, playing Christmas music and sipping hot cocoa around the fireplace. The snow fell hard and fast. Tanya's mom insisted everyone stay over since it was already late and the weather was getting rough. There was plenty of room, she said, and no one argued.

I slept in one of the guest rooms, wrapped up in a soft blanket, feeling thankful for where I was. Marcus slept in the den with Greg.

This year had been full of surprises, challenges, and changes—but right then, I was surrounded by laughter and love.

I woke up in the middle of the night to check on him. He wasn't asleep; instead, he was watching *It's a Wonderful Life* on his phone. I surprised him when I tapped his shoulder.

Marcus jumped. "What are you doing down here? Never mind, I know," he said as he sat up.

"You're going to sneak into the desserts." He laughed.

"No, I'm just checking on you," I said. "But that's not a bad idea."

He took my hands in his and gave them a gentle squeeze. "I never thought being stuck in a snowstorm would feel this good."

The lower part of my body tingled a little at the warmth from the friction of his palms. The entire house was silent; everyone was sleeping, and the Christmas lights that played Christmas carols cast soft colors across the room, like a secret glow meant only for us. And God, the way his thumb circled the inside of my palms... it sent heat curling low in my stomach and somewhere else. A part of me ached to slide under the blanket with him, to lay on top of him, and to feel his arms around me like that was where I belonged.

I wanted him so badly in that moment; to taste him, to make love to him slowly under this soft, magical hush of Christmas Eve. But it was too soon and too risky for my heart. Besides, we're in my best friend's parents' house, and everything between us was still delicate and blooming. I couldn't ruin that by letting desire lead me where my heart wasn't ready to admit it wanted to go.

I sighed. "I'm glad you're here, too. Also, what do you think about the movie?" I asked, trying to steady myself, trying to breathe like he wasn't unraveling me with his touch.

"It's really good for a black and white movie."

"They have it in color, too. I love both versions. And you really checked out my movie, aww!" I said, pursing my lips.

But inside, all I could think was how handsome he looked in the glow of the Christmas tree and lights that decorated the den. How gentle he was with me, and how if I wasn't careful, I could fall in love with him faster than the snow outside was falling. And some reckless part of me thought that wouldn't be a bad thing.

CHRISTMAS IN HARTFORD

I jumped out of bed Christmas morning, ran downstairs to say Merry Christmas to Marcus, and everyone else, too, but mainly Marcus. The smell of breakfast filled the air. "Mmm ... bacon, cinnamon rolls, and coffee. Merry Christmas, everyone," I said as I hit the living room and gave my man a hug and a kiss. Everyone had gathered around the tree waiting for Mrs. Daniels to call us in for breakfast.

Tanya clapped her hands and asked for everyone's attention. "I want to thank God for allowing us to spend Christmas Eve and Christmas day together. I know it's not Thanksgiving, but I would like to share what I'm thankful for if you guys don't mind."

We all told her to share in unison.

"First, I want to...wait...hold on, guys," she said, looking toward the direction of the kitchen. "Mama! Come into the living room for a minute, please," she hollered from the living room.

"Wait a minute, baby. Let me put this bacon on the tray," said Mrs. Daniels.

Mrs. Daniels entered the living room and sat on her husband's lap. He feigned like she was heavy and yelled

"Ouch!" and laughed. We all laughed, including Mrs. Daniels.

Tanya continued. "I'm blessed beyond measure to still have my parents in good health. I love you both. Thank you for treating my friends like family. Greg, I'm thankful our mothers are world-class busybodies. Only they could treat our love lives like a joint project and somehow force us to reconnect. I'm curious to see where this goes, especially since you're just a couple of hours from Chicago and they can't 'accidentally' arrange surprise visits.

Marcus, I'm thankful for the joy you've brought into my girl's life. And, Jenny, I'm thankful that we became friends in law school after that incident that we shall not mention." She looked at me with squinted eyes.

Mrs. Daniels and I fell out laughing. Everyone else looked at each other wondering what we were laughing about.

"Any who, Jenny, you're my best friend for life. I will continue to support you, push you, love you, and there's nothing you can do about it!" she finished as tears poured down her cheeks.

The second her voice broke, something inside me cracked wide open. I crossed the room without even thinking my legs moved before my mind caught up, and I wrapped her in a full, warm bear hug. Her arms flew around me, holding on tight like she would never see me again.

Her tears soaked into my shoulder, and I felt mine spill over onto her, sliding down my cheeks.

Her body trembled against mine, and I tightened my hold, rocking us side to side to comfort us both.

I could feel her soul, the bond between us settle even deeper, like roots digging into the earth. As I held her and rubbed the back of her head, all I could think of was how lucky I am to have Tanya as my true ride or die. A friend who loved me fiercely, and how I'd follow her to the ends of the earth if she ever needed me to.

She pulled back. "Okay. Okay. Let's all go wash up for breakfast," said Tanya.

"I hadn't said breakfast was ready," said Mrs. Daniels.

"Mama, how much longer before breakfast?" asked Tanya.

"It's ready," said Mrs. Daniels. Everyone laughed.

"Maaaama!" she said.

"I say when breakfast is ready." Mr. Daniels walked over and patted her butt. "Now, everyone go wash up for breakfast."

After we ate a delicious breakfast, we returned to the living room. Tanya handed out gifts, and we took turns opening them while carols played on the TV. Marcus gave me a silver bracelet with a tiny heart charm, and when I looked up at him, he just smiled and said, "Something simple to remember this Christmas by."

Later, as I checked my phone, I saw a text from Jeremy that read, *Merry Christmas, Jenny.* I stared at it for a second, then rolled my eyes and set my phone face down on the couch. That chapter was closed, and I had no desire to reopen it. The rest of the day was perfect; full of love, good food, and the peace that only comes when you're surrounded by people who make you feel at home. It was without a doubt a Christmas I'd never forget.

New Year's Day

Time flew by, and suddenly it was New Year's Eve. Marcus and I spent the night with his mother. We snuggled and made googly eyes at each other in her warm and cozy living room. The fireplace crackled as Marcus held me tight, kissing my neck. "I hate that you have to go back to Chicago," he murmured.

I shifted in his arms just enough to see his face. The firelight painted his skin in warm tones, making his eyes look more enticing. "Don't say it like that," I whispered. "You're going to make me ugly cry in front of your mom's fireplace."

He gave a small, sad smile. "I'm serious, Jenny. This month with you... it felt like the best part of my year. Maybe the best part of a few years."

His confession sent chills throughout my body. "It's been the best part of mine too," I said. "I didn't expect any of this."

Marcus ran his thumb along my jaw. "I don't want this just to be a holiday thing. I don't care about distance. I don't care about timing. I care about you."

The words sank into me like warmth from the fire, spreading through every inch of me. "You really think we can make this work? Me in Chicago... you here?"

He nodded, no hesitation. "I think we already started making it work. The rest is just logistics."

I laughed softly. "You and your optimism."

He leaned his forehead against mine. "You bring it out of me."

For a moment, neither of us spoke. The only sounds were the soft pop of the firewood and my heartbeat.

"I wish I didn't have to leave," I admitted. The truth sat heavy in my chest.

His arms tightened around me. "Then give me something to hold onto until you get back."

I looked up at him. "What do you want?"

"A promise," he said. "That Chicago won't make you forget how this felt."

I cupped his cheek. "Marcus... there's no version of me that could forget this."

He exhaled a slow, relieved breath, and pulled me back to his chest as another log crackled and fell apart in the fire. Snow drifted quietly outside, and the entire room felt like it was holding its breath with us, waiting for the new year, for morning, for whatever came next.

The Christmas tree was still up, its lights twinkling against the window as if it knew the holidays weren't quite ready to be over.

Marcus's mom had made a big pot of gumbo, and we sat around her dining table listening to her tell embarrassing stories about her son. I loved every bit of it. She told me about how he once tried to make cookies by himself and nearly set the kitchen on fire. I shared my embarrassing moments as well so he wouldn't feel too embarrassed. Marcus shook his head, smiling sheepishly, and I couldn't stop laughing. It felt like the room was echoing love, and I was right where I was supposed to be.

After dinner, his mother went to bed, leaving the two of us alone in the living room. The TV was on, counting down to midnight with all the New Year's Eve celebrations from New York. I took a quick look at the clock to check the time.

"It's already ten o'clock," I whispered. "In two hours, we'll be in a brand-new year. And in two days, I'll be heading back home."

Marcus looked at me with that calm confidence that always made my heart skip. "About that," he said, reaching behind the couch and pulling out a sleek black binder.

I frowned, curious. "What's this?"

He handed it to me and smiled. "Just ... something I've been working on."

When I opened it, I froze. Inside were real estate documents with my city, Chicago, listed all over them. At that instant, my jaw dropped. I looked again, my eyes widening as I saw his name and the name of the coffee shop printed across the top. "Wait a minute ... Marcus, what is this?"

He chuckled, rubbing the back of his neck. "It's a little secret I've been keeping. I'm not just a barista, Jenny. I actually own that coffee shop ... and one in Los Angeles... and another in Orlando."

I looked at him, completely speechless. "You ... own them?"

"Yep," he said, his smile widening. "And now, I want to open one in Chicago. I've already started the process, but I didn't want to move forward until I knew something was happening between us for sure."

I stared at him, still holding the documents in my lap. "I don't understand?"

He reached for my hand, his voice loving, and shared those heartfelt words I would never forget. "I'm falling in love with you, and I don't want to lose you. I think we both want something real. It has been years since I felt this way about anyone. I want to be wherever you are, Jenny. I want us to be exclusive. You and me."

My throat tightened, and before I could stop myself, tears had already welled up. "Marcus," I whispered, "you mean you're moving to Chicago?"

"I'm there if you'll have me." He stared deep into my soul.

I didn't even try to hide my excitement. My heart felt so full I thought it might burst. "Yes." My voice trembled. "Yes, Marcus, I want that too, and I'm falling in love with you."

We sat there grinning at each other like two teenagers with a secret no one else in the world could understand. His mother must have heard our laughter, because she came back out in her robe, her hair wrapped, smiling like she already knew what was going on. "What's all this joy I'm hearing out here?"

Marcus told her the news, and her eyes filled with happy tears. She came over and hugged us both. "I knew it," she said, squeezing me tight. "I told Marcus that one day, he'd find a woman who saw his heart and not just his hustle. And here you are."

I smiled and whispered, "Thank you, Mrs. Grace."

We spent the last few minutes before midnight reminiscing and sharing hopes for the new year. I excused myself for a moment and stepped into the kitchen to call my mom. When she picked up, I could already hear her smile through the phone. "Hey baby, Happy New Year!"

"Mom," I said, unable to keep the excitement out of my voice. "I just wanted to tell you ... Marcus and I are going to try to make it work. This has been the best Christmas: snow, falling in love, and finally finding peace in my life after my divorce. He's planning to come to Chicago and open a coffee shop there."

I could hear her clapping her hands, her laughter soft and sweet. "Oh, honey, I'm so happy for you! You deserve this, Jenny. You deserve to be loved by the right person."

"Thanks, Mom," I said, my eyes stinging a little. "I think I will be."

By the time I got back to the living room, the countdown had already begun.

"Ten! Nine! Eight!" he shouted.

Marcus stood grinning, holding out his hand to me. I took it and moved close to him.

We raised our voices and shouted, "Three! Two! One!" in excitement for what was coming in the New Year.

As the clock struck midnight, fireworks exploded on the TV screen, and Marcus grabbed me and kissed me. It was passionate and full of promise. His mother gasped playfully from the couch, laughing as she clapped her hands. "Happy New Year, my darlings."

When he pulled back, his forehead rested against mine. "Happy New Year, baby."

That was the first time he called me baby. "Happy New Year, baby," I repeated with love.

His mother came over and wrapped her arms around both of us. "Now that's the way to start a new year."

And at that moment, surrounded by all the love, I knew without a doubt this wasn't just the beginning of a new year. It was the beginning of the rest of my life with Marcus from Hartford.

Epilogue - Coming Next Christmas in Hartford Wedding

A year later, life looked beautiful and unbelievably different. Marcus and I had built something solid, something real. Between trips back and forth from Chicago and Hartford, our love grew in the spaces between airport gates, phone calls that lasted past midnight, and weekends where we met halfway just to spend two days together

The grand opening of Marcus's new coffee shop felt like a dream. The place was buzzing—warm lights strung across the ceiling, soft jazz playing in the background, the smell of espresso and caramel drifting through the air. People filled every corner: customers tasting samples, friends cheering him on, his mother fussing with the pastry display like it was her personal mission.

I was standing near the counter, helping hand out cups and trying not to cry from pure pride, when Marcus cleared his throat into the mic.

"Excuse me, everyone—can I get your attention for one second?"

The room quieted, people turning, cameras lifting as a few local bloggers and news folks angled in his direction. He looked nervous, but in the sweet, glowing way that made my heart trip over itself.

He smiled at the crowd... then looked straight at me.

"When he finally opened his new coffee shop in downtown Chicago, he surprised me at the grand opening with a ring—right there in front of a crowd of customers, cameras, and our closest friends. I said yes through tears, laughter, and with the smell of freshly brewed coffee filling the air."

But here's what happened between...

Marcus stepped out from behind the counter, wiping his palms on his apron like he was about to negotiate a million-dollar deal. The entire room followed his movements, a hush falling heavy and warm.

"Jenny," he said, his voice trembling just enough to make my knees go soft. "You said yes to a snowed-in Christmas with me. You said yes to long-distance. You said yes to believing in something new again." He swallowed, eyes shining. "So now... I'm hoping you'll say yes one more time."

My breath caught as he reached into his pocket. The crowd let out a collective gasp—somebody whispered, "Oh my God, he's doing it."

And then he was kneeling. Right there on the polished concrete floor between sacks of beans and a crowd of strangers who suddenly felt like family.

He opened the tiny velvet box, and the diamond caught the light from the café's pendant lamps, throwing a sparkle across his face.

"Jenny Thompson," he said softly, like the words were a prayer, "will you marry me?"

Everything inside me burst—my heart, my breath, my composure. Tears spilled so fast I didn't even try to stop them. Laughter bubbled out of me at the same time because of course this man would propose to me in a coffee shop, surrounded by espresso machines and oat-milk lattes. It was so perfectly him.

"Yes," I choked out, nodding so hard the crowd laughed. "Yes! Marcus... yes."

He slid the ring onto my shaking finger as the entire shop erupted into applause—customers cheering, friends screaming, his mother waving a napkin like a victory flag. The smell of freshly brewed coffee surrounded us, warm and rich, and he stood, pulling me into his arms as cameras flashed and someone shouted, "Kiss her!"

So he did—right there in the middle of the shop he built from scratch, with the man I loved tasting faintly of espresso and hope.

And it felt like the start of the rest of our lives.

Now, here we were—back in Hartford, the place where it all started.

Snowflakes fell softly outside Tanya's parents' home as I stood by the window, clutching my mug of cocoa and staring at the calendar. Two weeks until Christmas. Two weeks until our wedding day.

"Girl, why do you look like that?" Tanya asked, walking in with a plate of cookies. "You look like somebody just told you Santa canceled Christmas."

I laughed, running a hand through my hair. "Because it feels like everything's happening all at once! The caterer called and said the cake design got mixed up, Marcus's tux isn't ready, and your mama said the florist delivered tulips instead of poinsettias."

Tanya rolled her eyes. "It wouldn't be a real wedding if something didn't go wrong. Don't worry, we'll fix it. You just focus on not passing out before you walk down that aisle."

I smiled, taking a deep breath. "You're right. I just... can't believe it's actually happening. I'm marrying Marcus Porter."

Tanya grinned. "That man has been crazy about you since you first walked into his coffee shop. This was bound to happen."

Later that evening, Marcus and I met at his mom's bakery to go over last-minute plans. She'd insisted on baking our wedding cake herself, and the smell of vanilla and sugar filled the air. Marcus looked as handsome as ever, leaning against the counter, watching me with that same soft smile he always gave when I was stressing out.

"You know," he said, walking over and taking my hand, "no matter what happens—the flowers, the cake, the tux—none of it really matters. As long as we say 'I do,' that's all I care about."

I laughed, leaning into him. "You're just saying that because you're not the one who had to pick between eight shades of ivory."

He kissed my forehead. "You could walk down that aisle in pajamas, Jenny, and I'd still think you were the most beautiful woman in the world."

I swatted his arm, blushing. "You better stop before I forget all about this cake tasting."

He chuckled, with that deep, warm laugh I'd fallen in love with. "Promise me one thing," he said, looking at me seriously now. "When all the chaos hits—and it will—you'll remember this moment. You'll remember that this is supposed to be fun. It's supposed to be us."

I smiled and nodded. "I promise."

Outside, the snow fell thicker, blanketing Hartford in white. The bells from the church down the street echoed faintly through the night, and I couldn't help but think—this was where our story began, and soon, it would be where we'd start the rest of our lives together.

And even though planning the wedding felt like juggling mistletoe and madness, I wouldn't trade it for the world. In just a few short days, I'd be walking down that aisle toward the man who made Christmas in Connecticut feel like home.

Not the end...but to be continued.

About the author

G.P. Jackson is the pen name for Geletta Shavers, who is a social worker, mental health therapist, and author who uses her voice to empower, provoke, and sometimes terrify. Known for chilling stories that burrow deep into the human psyche, Geletta blends real-world emotional insight with supernatural suspense in *Dragged Into Darkness*. Her years in mental health give her a rare perspective on fear, trauma, and survival — themes that pulse through every page.

In addition to horror and thrillers, Geletta created a powerful self-care journal for women under her pen name, Ms. G, LCSW. Whether guiding women toward healing or pulling readers into dark fictional worlds, she believes in the power of storytelling to confront the truth and sometimes, to escape it.

Other titles by Geletta Shavers include *The Inheritance of Amaya Montgomery*, *Loving Myself First:*

My Self-Care Journal. Dragged into Darkness, and a spicy romance-Twisted Desire: In too Deep.

If you would like to connect with me, please visit:

Instagram: author_geletta_123

YouTube: Geletta Shavers, LCSW

https://www.facebook.com/profile.php?id=61564210504377

Made in the USA
Coppell, TX
20 January 2026

68832609R00056